EVERYWHERE

Written by Adam Loveless
Illustrated by Madeline Timm

First printing edition, 2021

Everywhere
Written by Adam Loveless
Illustrated by Madeline Timm

ISBN 978-0-578-76561-7 (hardback)

Published by:
Loveless Letters
Houston, TX, USA

To my air - Oli and Cora
-AL

To Scout, who always wants to pick the white dandelions.
-MT

A mother, a father, a daughter and son,
were off to bed after a day of fun.
The kids jumped in bed, and said their good nights,
gave hugs and kisses, and turned off the lights.

ut just before Mom and
ad could sneak out,
he little ones together
ave out a shout.
Mommy and Daddy -
lease come sit!
tay here with us,
ust for a bit."

They walked back in and sat on the beds,
then gently stroked the children's' heads.
"Listen," Mom said, "When you feel on your own, we're
always close by, you are never alone."

"Look outside," Dad chimed in,
"What do you see?
The moon shining back, as bright as can be?
We asked the moon to shine real bright,
to be with you both, throughout the whole night."

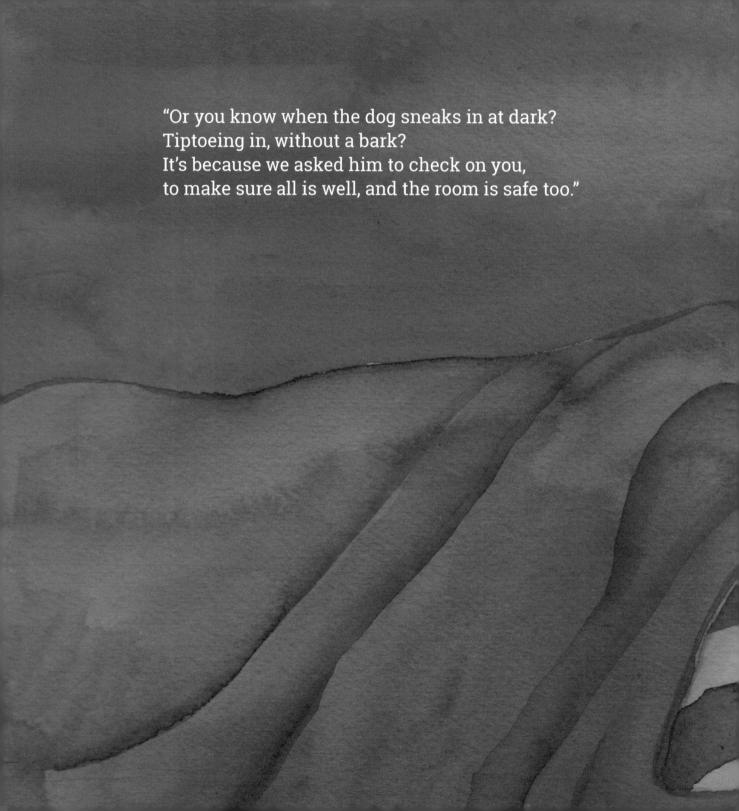

"Or you know when the dog sneaks in at dark?
Tiptoeing in, without a bark?
It's because we asked him to check on you,
to make sure all is well, and the room is safe too."

"Plus," Mom said, "This idea isn't just for the night.
No, we're even with you both during the daylight.
Outside, at school...even on the playground.
Just look closely, we're always around."

"But how will be know?" asked the girl with a sigh.
"Just look for a red bird that lands close by,"
Dad explained, "It's not by chance, it knows you two.
We told the bird the great things you both do."

"Or when you both see a dandelion,
and all the white flurries start to go flyin',"
Mom said, "Each one is a wish we sent your ways,
to brighten every moment of both of your days."

"Or perhaps the day's done, and the sun's off to bed.
We'll ask the sunset to add some bright red.
Your favorite color, that's what you'll see,
because that's what we wished for it to be."

"And even later when you're both all grown, you'll be taller, wiser, and living on your own." Dad explained, "If things don't go according to plan, you can rely on us to lend a helpful hand."

"Like if you're in a race,
and your legs starts slowing,"
Mom said, "We'll send a cool breeze
to keep you going."

"Or perhaps you're driving, and your favorite song comes on.
That's us wanting for you to dance along."

"Or even if there's a dark, rainy day,
with sad feelings that just won't go away.
We'll ask for a rainbow to appear in the sky,
to make you look up, and hold your head up high."

"A gleeful moment, a happy thought.
A flower in a random spot.
A skipped heartbeat, a breath-taking view.
The smell of cookies all around you."

"We hope these things
help remind you of,
our endless, forever,
never-aging love.
So rest your heads, my dears,
there is nothing to fear.
For from now and forever,
we'll always be here."

As the lights were about to be turned off,
the little boy stirred, and gave a small cough.
"Mom & Dad, what about me?
I want to help, what can I be?"

They both smiled and said to their son,
"That's a good question...but an easy one.
You and your sister...you both are the air.
Because to Mom and Dad...you are everywhere."

CPSIA information can be obtained
at www.ICGtesting.com
Printed in the USA
LVHW071734310521
688954LV00001B/4